George

Jules Feiffer

Michael di Capua Books

SCHOLASTIC INC.

New York Toronto London Auckland Sydney
Mexico City New Delhi Hong Kong

To Madeline

ISBN 0-439-21018-6

Copyright © 1999 by Jules Feiffer.
All rights reserved.
Published by Scholastic Inc., 555 Broadway, New York, NY 10012, by arrangement with Harper Collins Publishers.
SCHOLASTIC and associated logos are trademarks and/or registered trademarks of Scholastic Inc.

12 11 10 9 8 7 6 5 4 3 2 1   0 1 2 3 4 5/0

Printed in the U.S.A.   08

First Scholastic printing, October 2000

Designed by Steve Scott.

George's mother said:

"Bark, George."

George went: "Meow."

"No, George," said George's mother.
"Cats go meow. Dogs go arf.
Now, bark, George."

George went: "Quack-quack."

"No, George," said George's mother.
"Ducks go quack-quack. Dogs go arf.
Now, bark, George."

George went: "Oink."

"No, George," said George's mother.
"Pigs go oink. Dogs go arf.
Now, bark, George."

George went: "Moo."

George's mother took George to the vet.

"I'll soon get to the bottom of this," said the vet.

"Please bark, George."

George went: "Meow."

The vet reached deep down inside of George . . .

And pulled out a cat.

"Bark again, George." George went: "Quack-quack."
The vet reached deep, deep down inside of George . . .

And pulled out a duck.

"Bark again, George." George went: "Oink."
The vet reached deep, deep, deep down inside of George . . .

And pulled out a pig.

Then he reached deep, deep, deep, deep, deep, deep, deep, deep, deep, deep, deep down inside of George . . .

And pulled out a cow.

"Bark again, George."

George went:

arf

George's mother was so thrilled that she kissed the vet . . .

And the cat. And the duck. And the pig. And the cow.

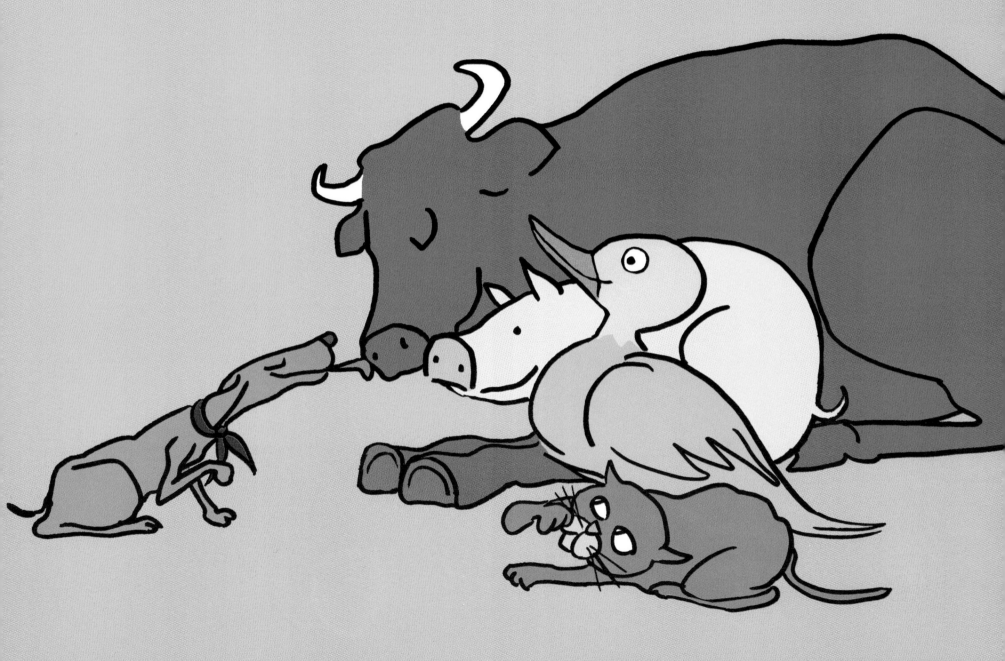

On the way home, she wanted to show George off
to everyone on the street. So she said, "Bark, George."

And George went:

ISBN 0-439-22790-9

EAN

9 780439 227902

SCHOLASTIC INC.   **$3.99 US**

This
edition
is only
available for
distribution
through the
school market.